James Harris Malmesbury

The Voice of Truth to the People of England

James Harris Malmesbury

The Voice of Truth to the People of England

ISBN/EAN: 9783337409098

Printed in Europe, USA, Canada, Australia, Japan

Cover: Foto ©Andreas Hilbeck / pixelio.de

More available books at **www.hansebooks.com**

THE

VOICE OF TRUTH, &c.

THE

VOICE OF TRUTH

TO THE

PEOPLE OF ENGLAND,

OF ALL

RANKS AND DESCRIPTIONS,

ON OCCASION OF

LORD MALMESBURY'S RETURN

FROM

LISLE.

" Go, call thy Sons, inftruct them what a Debt
·" They owe their Anceftors, and make them fwear
" To pay it, by tranfinitting down, intire,
" Thofe facred Rights, to which themfelves were born."

AKENSIDE.

RIGHT HON. WILLIAM WINDHAM,

SECRETARY AT WAR, &c. &c.

SIR,

HAD the following sheets been written some months ago, they would have been laid, where every book on such a subject ought to be laid, at the feet of *Mr. Burke.* But as it has pleased God to snatch him from a world that was not worthy of him, there is no one to whom it so properly belongs, as to Him on whom that great man dying, *cast his mantle.*

a   I shall

I shall, perhaps, be suspected of a vain display of taste, when I profess how much I venerate the author of the Letters on a Regicide Peace.—*Ille se multum in literis proficisse sciat, cui Cicero Valde placuerit.* But surely, Sir, it is no pretension to taste, to admire that of which none could be insensible. His splendid wit—his uncommon reasoning faculties—his penetration and sagacity—his deep knowledge in all the provinces of nature and of science, and all the accomplishments which may make it truly said of him,

Ingenium cui Diis et Mens contermina Cœlo
Cuncta unus, cunctos qui super unus erat.

To say nothing of his honour, his integrity, his virtue and magnanimity, were qualities too obvious to escape the most superficial observer. To use the words of a great man, " The Eternal Spirit, who can enrich with all utterance and knowledge, sent out his seraphim with the hallowed fire of

of his altar, to touch and purify his lips."
The poſſeſſor of theſe qualities is, alas, no
more; yet muſt the ſenſe of their value ever
remain impreſſed upon our hearts : and
though the ſpace which he filled, as a man,
in our affections, and as an author, in the
world of letters, muſt ever remain a hope-
leſs void, it is no ſmall conſolation to the
country, and no trifling pledge of the ſucceſs
of this little book, that, as a ſtateſman, his
loſs is not irreparable, ſince he has left behind
him a man, at once the moſt zealous patron
of his principles, and the moſt ample in-
heritor of his talents. To that man—to
you, Sir, I preſume to dedicate the following
ſheets, feeling myſelf, in common with all
the people of England, your debtor, admirer,
and humble Servant,

THE AUTHOR.

London, October, 1797.

THE

THE

VOICE OF TRUTH, &c.

My Countrymen,

THE die is caft—compromife is at an end—
there is now no retreat—now no other alternative but inftantly to affert the fpirit which was
once the boaft of Englifhmen, or foon to have the
name of Briton expunged from the current lan-
guage of the world, to be found only in the records
of antiquity, with the virtues which once accom-
panied it, and other terms equally obfolete and
forgotten. Fatally do you flatter yourfelves, if
you think you can be at once fafe and fupine;
if you hope to find fecurity in your fleeping trea-
fures; or, if you imagine that the ordinary re-
fources, which would have ferved in civilized times,

B

againſt a civilized enemy, will avail you now.
Your enemy fights for exiſtence; the conteſt is
not for territory—it is not for honours—it is for
exiſtence. Your enemy can live but by war; he
periſhes with peace. In him the order of nature
is reverſed; the poiſon of all other beings, to him
is nouriſhment. Your ſtruggle is with an uſurpa-
tion engendered by homicide, and fed by blood;
if he ſheath the ſword, he dies of inani-
tion; he will not ſeek annihilation. With him,
therefore, war muſt be co-exiſtent; to get rid of
one, you muſt extinguiſh the other. You have
no other choice, but either to ſubmit your necks to
the deteſted, and once deſpiſed yoke of France;
or elſe to open the armoury of your anceſtors, take
down the mail, which in a degenerate hour commerce, and vice, and luxury had conſigned to ruſt
and deriſion; and evince to the world, that you
have yet vigour to wield them.

Accurſed be thoſe who fill the air with deluſive
ſounds to cheat your ſenſes, and divert from
the proſpect before you; thoſe pandars who abet
the plan of ſeduction, and endeavour to ſink our
country to proſtitution and debaſement, in the polluted arms of France. Thoſe baſtard, degenerate
ſons of England, who would proſtrate all the

6   glories

glories fo hardly atchieved in Creffy, Agincourt, Blenheim, Minden and Quebec; all the laurels won by your Edwards and Henry's, your Marlborough and your Wolfe, your Blake, your Hawke and your Howe, at the feet of the worst refufe of that people from whofe brows they were torn. Can you forget the time when the fuppofition that France could dictate terms of Peace to England, would have been refented by the meaneft wretch that dragged exiftence through your ftreets? When your very women would have undertaken to chaftife the chattering infolence of France? And was all this but the coward exultation of profperity? Will Britons now meanly crouch to thofe they once brow beat and defpifed? Will they put it in the power of every fqualid Frenchman to retort their national boaft, and exultingly afk, *Now* is one Englifhman a match for two French!! Shall the fublime motto to this addrefs, and the patriotic ftrains of Thomfon, at whofe founds the hearts of Britons once fwelled with national pride, only remain records to prove to what a proud height your forefathers afpired, and to what abject humiliation you fuffered yourfelves to be debafed? Are you aware that all this and worfe, much worfe, awaits you, if you do not fummon all your fortitude, and

bring

bring the whole energy of your fouls into action? Temporifing, half meafures, will not fuffice—the whole man, and every limb, and every mufcle of the man, and all his means muft be called forth and put upon the ftrain; not only muft your bodily, but your intellectual force be exerted. You muft exact the moft rigid duty from your mind. The times demand extraordinary jealoufy, diftruft, and fufpicion on the one hand, and extraordinary confidence on the other, and in diftinguifhing whom you fhould truft, and whom fufpect, your judgment will be exercifed. You are not to fubmit to the hafty decifion which paffion, prejudice, or a too quick fenfe of the fhare you bear in the general calamity of the day, may pronounce; but appeal to the cool, unbiaffed judgment which diligent inveftigation, and a patient inquiry after truth, fhall enable you to form. In this inquiry you muft impartially attend to the legal advocates on both fides; but, fpurn from you thofe traitors, who, with the counterfeit coin of revolution, confifcation, and their parents the *Rights of Man*, would bribe you to betray your duty, and facrifice yourfelves.

Let me repeat it to you, you muft look your fituation boldly in the face, or neceffarily fall like cowards.

cowards. The times are infinitely more critical than any of which we have an account in hiſtory. Your danger is great; but the magnitude of the danger, if duly meaſured and acted upon, may become the means of ſafety and of honour. Providence may have appointed it to rally back the old ſpirit of Britain, long ſunk in the enervating embraces of commerce and luxury. A field lies before you fit for heroes to run the courſe of honour in, to grapple manfully with ſuch difficulties will be glorious whether you riſe or fall. They are greater than any of thoſe your forefathers had to encounter, ſince the time of the Norman conqueſt; had they your cauſe to prick them on, they would have ſtruck a blow, of which after-ages would have heard with aſtoniſhment; but they always ſecured their honour; defeat was to them an unuſual ſound; ſubmiſſion they knew not; under the perſuaſion that Engliſhmen were invincible, they actually became ſo; do you alſo remain ſteady to that belief, and you will not fail to realize it—If you fall ſhort—your caſe is deſperate.

You muſt therefore, my countrymen, indeed you muſt, prepare to dare every thing, or ſink to nothing—to hazard much, or ſuffer all.—To
Engliſh-

Englishmen it would be superfluous to recommend valour, if valour consisted only in a prodigal disregard of life; but it has many distinct branches, with as many distinct names, to all of which I will give that one of valour, as most dear, and most attractive to the hearts of Britons. Know, then, that there is a portion of valour, and that of the most dignified kind, in every sacrifice you make at the shrines of honour, probity or virtue. It often requires more courage to subdue an unworthy passion, than to break a lance with a foe. I fear you will have occasion to try your spirit frequently in this respect.—As you would risk your life in battle, in order afterwards to enjoy it securely, you must yield up much of your present ease to insure your future peace, and sacrifice a portion of your present wealth to the security of your permanent property. Believe me, my countrymen, without a liberal, an almost prodigal exertion of all those implements of defence, you will not long have peace, property, or life to defend; unless indeed you are willing, which I will not believe, to hold life, without property or peace, as ignominious vassals to the upstart usurpers, and fierce domination of France.

My

My national partialities and prejudices will not allow me to part with the hope, that you will feel the force of this appeal, and be prompt to act upon it. Fraud and deception may have had a temporary fuccefs in their efforts to blind you, but when Englifhmen once fee an object, they fee it clearly, and have only to underftand the right fide of a queftion in order to embrace it. You have had too many teachers on one fide, attend a little to one on the other. You have heard much about the people's rights; hearken to a few words about their duties.

It cannot, it ought not, to be concealed from you—your fituation is full of peril; you have not lefs to fear at home than abroad; nay you have more, your internal enemies are many, and are the more dangerous, becaufe fufpected but by few, and hard to be diftinguifhed from friends. Interwoven in the fabric of fociety, they occupy their fpace, and by a fuperficial eye are undiftinguifh-able from the reft, while like rotten threads they weaken the whole web, and rob it of its value. I repeat, it is not in France your worft, or only enemies are to be found; you breathe the fame air, you dip in one difh, you drink from one cup with traitors: they walk in your ftreets, they mix

in

in your focieties, they harangue in your clubs, and are to be found every where but in your churches.

There are enemies of another kind too; enemies that work by flow but certain, becaufe inceffant operation—enemies that not only ftimulate to wrong, but poifon the very fource of right—the heart. Your long cherifhed bofom friends, you carry them to your pillow without apprehenfion or diftruft; you hug the vipers to your bofom, and fleep in confcious fecurity while they imperceptibly moulder away the pillars upon which your happinefs is built; thofe muft be fhaken off, elfe your arms fall nervelefs; France overpowers you, and, too late for redrefs, you will difcover their treachery: the moft deceitful and dangerous charms that ever hung round the neck of man, and deluded him into mifery and difhonour, are avarice and voluptuoufnefs: would you efcape utter ruin now, fhake them from you.

I have faid that Englifhmen have only to fee, in order to purfue what is right. To them the difficulty is, *to know*, not *to do*. And yet it appears to me, that the road of duty and of honour lies before you plain, open, and obvious; you are only confounded by the fyren allurements of thofe who

would

would feduce you into the path of deftruction. If you have not penetration to difcover their trea-chery, nor fortitude to reject their follicitations till you are frighted off by conviction, embrace at once that conviction which reafon and common fenfe offer, and do not wait for that, which, late and fatal, will make repentance fruitlefs. Rather take it from the lips of fincerity now, than wait to receive it from the perfuafion of French bayonets, or the patriotic doctrine of the guillotine.

Oppofed to your ancient, eternal, and invete-rate enemy France in front, you ftand between two fets of men and opinions, each of which profeffes to guide you, and point out the path you ought to purfue. One urges you to ground your arms and run, the other exhorts you to ftand firm to your poft : one affures you, that the French are your friends ; the other bids you beware of their friendfhip, as more fatal than their enmity : one points out to you the laft five years of French hiftory as an example for you to imitate, and a fubject to admire ; the other bids you take a retrofpective view of the hiftory of your fore-fathers, and eftimate the value of their principles by the fruits they have produced ; of which you now tafte the fweets. The one is the body, whofe

C   conduct

conduct and principles intitle them to the name of
Jacobins; the other the government at large.
The Whigs I put out of the queftion, becaufe,
though hoftile to the minifter, they are not friends
to the French; and though, from erroneous no-
tions, defirous of fome immediate internal change,
they are not enemies to the Conftitution.

Viewing then, thefe two parties, if there be
among you any of fuch impenetrable hearts and
muddy underftandings as to hefitate between them,
I exhort fuch perfons, before they rufh into the
arms of their feducers, or give effect to their purpofes by delaying to decide, to examine fairly the
pretenfions of both. Let them at leaft, before
they adopt the doctrines of their new affociates,
be fure that their old advifers and protectors are
incompetent any longer to advife. This will be a
tafk of no great labour or difficulty; it lies within
the compafs of a nutfhell; the meaneft intellect
can comprehend it; fatuity, frenzy, or corruption
alone, can vitiate your decifion.

Obferve, my Countrymen, I fet out with de-
precating the erroneous notion that this is a time
for confidering whether the war were originally well
or ill founded; whether it were a matter of choice
or

or neceſſity: whether it were or were not miſcon-
ducted. If it were commenced in error, and miſ-
conducted in its progreſs, your duty to yourſelves
requires, that, now you are acting on the defenſive,
you ſhould exert your utmoſt vigour. Much
more, is it your duty, if, as might perhaps be
eaſily demonſtrated, the War originated on your
part in ſelf-defence.

Be that as it may, you are now at war, on the
defenſive, in very diſadvantageous circumſtances;
and the ſtake not leſs than exiſtence. It is now
your buſineſs to conſider, not how it began, but
how it ſhall end; not to debate whether in 1792
you committed an act of aggreſſion on France,
or ſhe on you, but whether in 1798 you will tamely
ſuffer yourſelves to be deſtroyed by France: not
to brood with fruitleſs lamentation, and vindictive
malignity over the calamities you have ſuſtained,
but to ſearch for means to ſecure your future ſuc-
ceſſes: not to load with obloquy and reproach
thoſe who, with good intentions, hazarded the
war, but to cruſh thoſe traitors who would make
peace the inſtrument of your ruin. I confeſs it is
probable, that there are among you ſome well
meaning men, who will yet find it difficult to diſ-
entangle themſelves from the net, in which the

craft

craft of your adverfaries have inmefhed their
judgment: who will have to deteft the fallacy of
fome propofitions which they have long taken for
granted, and to difmifs fome fancies to which time
and habit have given the folidity of opinion: after
having detected thofe impoftures, they will find
no difficulty in comprehending the extent of their
danger, and the duty it attaches on them.

If, on examining the two propofitions of pro-
tracted war on one hand, or ignominious peace on
the other, you find yourfelves incompetent to
decide from the materials now in your poffeffion;
and wifhing for advice, are confounded by the
adverfe opinions of two contradictory advifers,
your fafeft mode of procedure is to compare—and
on the comparifon judge between them—firft the
motives of each with that of the other, and,
fecondly, his abilities to advife. Along with this
make yourfelves mafters of the facts that govern
the queftion, and you can hardly be wrong in your
decifion.

Following the order in which I firft ftated them,
let us take a view of thofe who wifh you, by direct
fubmiffion to France, to intitle yourfelves to a par-
ticipation in the benefits and bleffings of endlefs
anarchy,

anarchy, fuch as that country has experienced in the laft five years: thefe are the Jacobins: and here you will have an advantage, for in examining the character of the men, you will comprehend the nature of their meafures, in which alone the former is defcribed. Do you wifh to know what a Jacobin is, you muft collect it from his actions, and the effects they have produced. No defcription can reach him: to comprehend him within the terms of an abftract definition, would be impoffible: Even Burke, that Briareus of intellect—muft fail in an attempt to define a phenomenon, in forming of which nature feems to have collected together, and compreffed into a mafs, all the ills with which original fin has curfed our nature—a monfter more hideous and deformed than morbid fancy ever pictured on the retina of a fever-frenzied brain. Not the bold invention of Shakefpeare, nor the fervid imagination of a *Teniers*, ever yet embodied a conception fo fublimely horrible: not the copious mind of our bard, when the wings of his all-pervading fancy fwept the vault of hell to find materials for the fpells of forcerers, ever dreamed of fuch a cauldron of ills as the bofom of a Jacobin; —fuch a varied complication of mifchief—fuch a combination of jarring principles impreffed into the fervice of crime. The deferted ftrength and

energy

energy of virtue executing the commands of vice —intellect sitting in grave council with all the turbulent and destructive passions—Genius tinging the murderer's poniard with poison, and Eloquence pronouncing eulogies on assassination—Prudence guiding the hand of blind Outrage to the object of violation—and Philosophy throwing new lights upon the science of insurrection, pointing out new sources of confiscation, and devising new modes of sacrilege, and new schemes of plunder.

If facts bear me out in this faint sketch, you will see, that you ought to listen to their advice indeed, not to follow, but to act in direct opposition to it; for you cannot conceal it from yourselves, that the views of such men can only be accomplished, by the abrogation of all laws—by the overthrow of the Constitution—by the annihilation of government, and all the murder, confusion, and bloodshed attending such a process.

But see how facts bear out this picture. Look to France where they are engraven in characters never to be effaced; where a monument, mountain size, composed of human skulls and bones, and cemented with human blood, rears its frightful head in commemoration of the feats of Jacobins.

If

If difguft and terror will allow you, caft an eye to the fcene that unhappy country has prefented for the laft five years; all the work of Jacobin hands. Its plains inundated with blood; its ftreets polluted with carnage; its moft beautiful and profperous cities ravaged, depopulated, and laid in ruins; its beft men exiled, their widows and orphans butchered; or worfe, configned to wafte away life in poverty and famine, in anguifh and difconfolation. Difcretionary power over life and death, delegated, in mockery of law, to the moft profligate and fanguinary of men, and not lefs than fifty thoufand prifons filled with pretended confpirators to fupply their butchery with materials to work upon. Every kind of moral excellence denounced as hoftile to the republic; every fpecies of moral depravity courted, nurfed, and encouraged. Talents, learning, virtue, probity, religion, perfecuted and profcribed—murder, robbery, impiety and atheifm openly avowed and publickly applauded. The minifters of religion butchered for celebrating the rites of their church, and affaffins received in full fenate, and for their magnanimity in producing part of a mutilated human body on the end of a pike, rewarded with *honourable men-tion*. Commerce, arts, and fcience extinguifhed; war and robbery only encouraged, the chaftity of

4

the fair fex violated at will; harmlefs women and maids, bribed with a promife of life to facrifice their honour to the luft of their judges, and the next moment delivered over to the hands of the executioner. Infancy, before it could conceive a criminal thought, and age, tottering on the very verge of death, feeble, impotent, and harmlefs, given to the blade of the guillotine, or the mercilefs claws of a mob, and huddled in one promifcuous indifcriminate flaughter with the vigorous, the bold, and the energetic. The guillotine plying its fhears, and the blood of its victims ftreaming on the cannibal fpectators of a puppet fhow below, who hailed the fhower with rapture, marking croffes on their forehead with it in ludicrous mimickry, and impious derifion of the rites of their church: a town converted to a fepulchre; every village a hecatomb of human facrifices—and murder having exhaufted its anger, doing its office in buffoonery and merriment. All for the rights of man, all for liberty and equality. All the work of Jacobins: the pretext liberty, the end, as you now know, defpotifm and flavery of the worft kind, and the moft hopelefs, becaufe *military*.

The government and laws which might have prevented fuch exceffes being diffolved; and the ſpirits of the French naturally volatile, vagrant, and licentious, being let loofe, they could not govern themſelves or their fortune; nor be reſtrained within the limits of that vaſt empire. Having drank deep of the intoxicating cup of licentiouſneſs, they refolved not to be niggards of it to others; and judiciouſly concluding that an example ſo very inviting as theirs would meet with imitators in every country, they haſtened to proclaim a kind of general ſaturnalia to be held at Paris; and invited all good citizens, who had no averſion to the taſte of human fleſh and blood, to repair thither and partake of the repaſt. To ſpeak leſs figuratively, all *Jacobins*, that is to ſay all who wiſhed to overturn their governments, to profcribe their religion, to murder their wealthy fellow citizens, and plunder them of their property; in ſhort to arm the phyſical ſtrength, againſt the talents and property of the refpective countries, were invited to repair to Paris, to fraternize, to enroll their names in the liſt of king-killers, and to take inſtruction and protection from thofe grave doctors of the new code. No ſooner was this magnetic power let abroad, than the attraction was felt by every particle of congenial matter, in all parts of Europe; in none more than England. Jacobin Societies met in London, and other parts

D

of England, and difpatched delegates to Paris, where they were received with favage exultation, felicitated on their nice fufceptibility, fraternized, kiffed, and inftructed. Thofe worthy Englifhmen having provided themfelves with a fufficiency of the infection to inoculate feven millions of people, if they could be prevailed upon to fubmit to the operation, returned home, and landed almoft under the cover of French guns; for to protect and facilitate their defigns, preparation was made for war, and foon after declared.

It is in this tranfaction you fee the point of contact between the French and Englifh jacobins—the fpot where the French fcyon was inferted in the Britifh ftock. If the Britifh jacobins have not proceeded to fuch exceffes as the French, you are not, on that account, to under-rate their intentions; you will wrong them very much by fuppofing that England would not have been put into as brifk motion as France, if they could have effected it. I affure you the fpirit was willing. Had it not been for the timely and vigorous exertions of your happy, protecting government, your fields would long before this have been fertilized with your own blood, and your rivers fwelled with the tears of your widows and orphans. As in France, the

people

people would have been thinned by the ferocious
contentions of ambitious equality-mongers. Those
who now difpenfe to you the benefits of good
order and laws, the bleffings of religion, the fweets
of courteous benevolence, and the tender confo-
lations of charity, would long before now have
fallen under the knife of the affaffin or executioner;
and thofe who have fwelled the catalogue of Old
Bailey convictions would be commanding you to
the field to fight their quarrels for power, and
harneffing one half of you like horfes to their ar-
tillery, to keep down the indignation of the other
half againft their betrayers. As certainly as all
this, and worfe, did pafs in France, fo certainly
would it have happened here : the fanatical admiration in which our jacobins hold their prototypes,
would not allow them, even, from motives of po-
licy, to deviate from their example, or conceal
their imitation. Perhaps we owe the mifcarriage
of their defigns to their open, indecent adoption,
not only of the plans, but of the arrangements,
forms, and barbarous technicals of their originals;
nay, of their very names. Thofe of you who do
not already know the fact, will find it difficult to
believe that there were Britons—I would rather
fay, men born in England, for Britons they were
not, who had their children (I was near faying

D 2   chriftened,

chriftened, but that would be blafphemous) named *Marat*, Robefpierre, &c. &c. in Shandean hope, that the virtues and glories of thofe names would influence their morals and fortune. Would men, adopting with fuch fervile imitation, the forms of the French jacobin's proceedings, abate an atom of the fubftance, wherein their advantage more effentially lay; no, no, in the fervour of fuch fanaticifm they would moft religioufly obferve the precepts and practice of their idols, and, if occafions did not naturally occur, they would force them, in order to evince the fidelity of their refemblance.

A circumftance naturally falls in here fo ftrongly demonftrative, not only of the Revolution, which the example of France had brought about in the hearts of thofe jacobins, but of the taint the public mind had received, and the influence it had upon the people of this country, that I muft remind you of it. Not content with calumniating the government, and vilifying the conftitution, the Jacobins openly difplayed a bafe, inveterate, unnatural averfion to the country and to yourfelves—in the fame fpirit of fanaticifm with which they worfhipped France, they execrated and anathematized England, avowing a rooted contempt and averfion to every thing Englifh, depreciating the un-

derftanding

derftanding of Englifhmen, maligning and deny-
ing even their courage, and calling in queftion
that which never before was doubted—the valour
of our armies, and the valour of our fleets—witnefs it all Europe! Britifh jacobins, men of deep
penetration and knowledge, were the firft who
ever called in queftion the valour of Britifh foldiers
and failors ;—but why ? Becaufe they well knew
that courage is as much and as often the refult of
opinion, fentiment, and habit of thinking, as of
material animal organization; and that diffemi-
nating the opinion that Britifh foldiers and failors
were not valiant, would have an ultimate tendency
to render them cowards, and make them an eafier
prey to France. There is another, and an obvious
reafon—when they faid Britifh foldiers and failors
were not brave, they were the dupes of their own
wifhes, and being wicked enough to wifh that it
were fo, were weak enough to believe it. But
how comes it to pafs that in England, a nation
fcarcely more remarkable for its valour, than its
pride of that valour, infomuch that a beggar,
being Englifh, would once have refented an im-
putation on the courage of his country, if offered
by a Peer of France, fuch grofs infulting, depreciating calumnies fhould be fuffered to pafs un-
punifhed. I will tell you ; becaufe the infection

of

of French wickednefs was fpreading; fome caught
it at once, fome by degrees, fome not at all.
Where the ear was allowed to hear, and the mind
permitted to digeſt, the firſt outworks of the
heart were taken : what, at firſt, created furprife,
when repeated, produced indifference and at laſt
ended in guilt. *Facilis defcenfus averni.*—One
act of compliance facilitates another, and every
ſtep we advance in vice diminiſhes our reluc-
tance, and accelerates our career. Once got
into the highway of all crime, jacobinifm—treafon,
parricide, ingratitude, and murder become familiar. Guard every avenue to your heart then, and
fince much, if not the whole of your former great-
nefs, was owing to your pride and honeſt prejudices,
look upon that man who attempts to deprive you
of them, with the cant of *Reafoning*, *Philofophy*,
and the *Rights of Man* in his mouth, as an inveterate enemy and a Jacobin, who wiſhes to ruin
you. Aſk him, in return, what is become of the
Rights of Frenchmen, and tell him you prefer your
old ruſty prejudices, to the rights which are con-
fined to five men out of twenty-eight million, and
to the reafoning and philofophy of a ſtanding army
—precifely to that have they brought things in
France.

Ah, my countrymen, if you have not yet parted with thofe fafeguards of your virtue—thofe honeft prejudices which fhed a mild luftre over our nature, and melt the harfhnefs of the human feature into the foft benignant lineaments of the angel; appeal to, and take the fentence of your hearts—not founded on the ftern, unrelenting principles of unmitigated democracy, which like its congenial vice, envy, knows no holiday, no pity, no remorfe; but, on the legitimate evidence of your own feelings, unfophifticated by jacobin artifice, unadulterated by the Rights of Man. State a cafe for the purpofe, fend it home to your heart, let it have entrance to the high court of confcience in your bofom, and not be kept *lingering* at the portal while the judge fleeps upon the bench. Fix your mind upon that man whom you moft love, moft admire, moft revere for his virtues; a man, rendered dear to your heart and venerable in your eyes, by majeftic fimplicity of character, by unfeigned piety, by a lively fenfe of juftice, by unremitted benevolence, by charity, difpenfing round a large fortune in chearful ftreams of beneficence to the children of forrow; fuppofe him before a felf-created court, compofed of fuch men among us as expiate the moft atrocious crimes, by the moft fhameful death; arraigned of the high

crimes

crimes and misdemeanors of weaith, talents, and virtue, and on the evidence of his character, convicted of those crimes; suppose him instantly delivered into the hands of a ferocious villain, who drags him to execution, aggravating murder and injustice with indignity—his mangled headless trunk denied a grave, and cast into the water to fatten the monsters of the deep: Suppose that by an extraordinary act of merciless lenity his widow and children were left alive, and you saw them, covered with rags, emaciated with hunger, melting under the corrosion of grief and despair, begging alms at the door of that cottage which their beneficence had formerly raised for the shelter of distress.

Suppose a minister of your religion, cloathed in the meek sanctity of his office, the affection and respect with which his virtues and instruction had first inspired you, improved to awful veneration by the hand of time, which, true to its trust, never fails to illustrate and render visible the foul, shedding a thousand glories upon the furrowed face of virtuous age; a man from whom yourself, and your father, perhaps your father's father, had imbibed the first principles of virtue, and received the consolations of our blessed religion, while you hung with rapture, on wisdom and piety,
dropping

dropping from his lips. Suppofe an infuriate mob of fiends in human fhape, hot from a banquet of blood, and flaming with the fanatical rage of atheifm, hunting him down with favage yells through the ftreets, feizing him, tearing from his temples the white hair, and fcattering it in the wind, buffeting his aged meek venerable face, trampling him under their feet, rending his feeble frame in pieces—the laft office of his tongue, a petition to Heaven to forgive them.

Or, fuppofe an old warrior, (fay Lord Howe) who had fpent the whole of his life in your defence, regardlefs of perfonal fafety, regardlefs of his eafe, enduring the toils and horrors of night ftorms and winter tempefts, encountering the extremes of climate, and expofing himfelf to your enemy whenever called upon: even in the wane of life, when age, or the decay of a conftitution, prematurely facrificed to the fervice of his country, called for repofe, entering with all the alacrity and vigour of youth upon new dangers to ferve you. Suppofe him called upon by a mob of bloody rebels, red from the flaughter of his Sovereign, and ordered by them to tarnifh all his glories, by tearing the badge of honour from his head, and putting in its ftead that of rebellion, and for refuling fufing to comply, inftantly torn to pieces; thofe limbs which brought glory, power, wealth, and fecurity to your fhores, and terror to thofe of your enemy, fcattered piecemeal in the air, and given to the birds and the beafts to devour.

What would be your feelings? Determine with yourfelves while yet you are unjacobinifed, while yet you are unimbued with the principles of *fanguinary political juftice*, and let your determination remain on record in your bofoms, to bear witnefs againft you hereafter, if hell fhould let loofe its vengeance fo far againft you as to corrupt you into Jacobins. Could you now endure fuch a fcene? Can you bear it even in imagination? And yet let me tell you my beloved countrymen, thefe are but faint pictures of facts, facts which in innumerable inftances occurred in France, facts done by the inftructors, the employers, and the bofom friends of thofe who would give a part of their limbs now, that you would make peace with France on the worft poffible terms. Such was the fate of very many of their moft learned and moft pious clergy. Such was the fate of feveral of their Generals who had retired in feeble old age and mutilation, to wafte the fhort remnant of life in the country round Paris. Such was the

6

fate

fate of the Duc de Rochefoucault, one of the firſt promoters of the Revolution, the reward of his confidence in a modern philoſopher and politician— Condorcet: and ſuch would have been the fate, if there had been a Revolution in England, of every man who had wealth, talent, or virtue, to make him an object of jacobin ſlaughter. Such would be the fate of the Duke of Bedford, of Earl Fitzwilliam, and of Mr. Fox, as ſurely as of Mr. Pitt, or Mr. Wyndham, ay, or of the immortal Burke, who compriſed within himſelf every power of the mind, every affection of the ſoul, every virtue, every feeling, and every endowment but wealth, that could make him the firſt victim of a jacobin inquiſition.

But is it not extraordinary, that jacobiniſm ſhould yet live, when the pretext upon which it was grounded, and the principles upon which it was defended, are cut up by the root: like ſome ſnakes, its jaws move, and contain their poiſon, after its body is cut in pieces: as vivacious as it is pernicious, it flouriſhes and bloſſoms on the head, after bark and root are cut away: like Richard in the play, " it is itſelf alone." Even the poiſon tree of Japan would die, if its root and bark were ſeparated from it; but while it lives beyond the

courſe

courfe of nature, its living ferves an ufeful purpofe, and fuggefts one queftion, an anfwer to
which will ferve as an antidote to the poifon, or at
leaft prevent its fpreading farther.

Qu. Were plunder, and rebellion, and murder
ufed by the Jacobins as the means of eftablifhing
the *Rights of Man*, or were the *Rights of Man*
made a pretext for plunder, murder, and rebellion? By Rights of Man, I mean, that principle
of *Liberty and Equality*, of which fo much has been
faid here, and in France, the laft feven years.

In tracing the whole fucceffion of tyrannies and
ufurpations which have followed clofe, each upon
the heels of the other, in that devoted country, it
would be hard to find any long interval in which
they had more liberty, or more equal diftribution
of rights or property, (I put juftice out of the
queftion) than in the worft day of the worft mo-
narchical defpotifm. The black cloud which hung
over it, during the defpotifm of that monfter
Robefpierre, was at beft gilded with the hope, but
no more, of future liberty. The chaos which fuc-
ceeded the deftruction of the monarchy had not
been reduced to form; nor had any mode of government affumed the fhape, and obtained the

fanction of law; yet it was a heavy, cruel defpotifm; and, in its cruelty, carried its overthrow
along with it: but the Jacobins were the partifans,
the fupporters, and the advocates of Robefpierre,
and of the Rights of Man. The Directory, however, has eitablifhed, and got into peaceable and
permanent poffeffion of a defpotifm of a worfe
kind than any of the Monarchies: it is not an in-
road on the practical part of the conftitution; it is
a complete overthrow and dereliction of the very
principle upon which it, and all their proceedings,
from the beginning, were founded. They dif-
qualify by force, and tranfport, without fo much as
the form of trial, fifty-two of the reprefentatives
of the people; and to fhew that they do not mean
to fubject the matter to frefh trial or difcuffion,
they affect to keep intire the Conftitution they have
violated. They do not fay, " this is a defective
" Conftitution, and therefore we annul it for the
" good of the people." No; but they tell the
people, " this is a good Conftitution, becaufe we
" can violate it, and therefore we will preferve it
" intire for our own purpofes, and violate it when-
" ever it fuits our convenience." In fhort, the
Directory are King, Legiflators, Judges, and Exe-
cutioners in one body; and, fo long as they have
a mercenary army to fupport them in their ufur-

pation,

pation, Liberty and Equality, and the Rights of Man, will lie dormant. So much for this new-fangled doctrine, and its comfortable effects on human happinefs; and fuch will always be the end of the fovereign power being wrefted into the hands of the people.—After committing millions of murders with it, (in this of France above three millions) they fink under the defpotifm of fome tyrannical ufurper. YOU SEE THEREFORE THAT LIBERTY, EQUALITY, AND THE RIGHTS OF MAN, ARE BUT PRETEXTS FOR USURPATION, CONFISCA-TION AND MURDER.

Turn your eyes now to the Englifh Jacobins, and fee how confiftently they have followed their leaders, and adhered to the doctrines of the Rights of Man, and with what fidelity they have, at the fame time, paid homage to ufurpation, in what-ever form or perfon it appeared.

They began with an attempt to tranfplant that baleful root of all evil into Britifh foil; and, for that purpofe, openly attacked your old, glorious, happy Conftitution, and ridiculed it as a fyftem of flavery, declaring, in unqualified terms, through the refolutions of their *enlightened* Committees, that Government was an ufurpation of the rights

of

of the people, and its adminiſtration criminal and corrupt. Nay; they went ſo far as to *denounce the American Conſtitution, becauſe it* bore ſome reſemblance to the Britiſh; or, to uſe their own words, becauſe it paid too much reſpect, and gave *too much protection to property.*

Having uſed thoſe, and various other ſtratagems, to delude the people, and finding that Engliſhmen were not to be cajoled with ſuch ſenſeleſs traſh, becauſe they had always been a free people, and knew the proper meaning and value of liberty; and being alſo convinced, that they ſtill remained firmly attached to their King and Conſtitution, the Jacobins, with that facility peculiar to them, wheeled about, changed their battery, and took refuge under that very Conſtitution they had, but juſt a day before, endeavoured to deſtroy: and concluding that they could not carry the Conſtitution by aſſault, they ſet induſtriouſly to work to ſap it, by pointing out ſuppoſed abuſes, and by calling aloud for parliamentary reform. Their attempts to deſtroy the Conſtitution gave it an acceſſion of ſtrength in the opinion of the people, who had the happineſs to ſee, in their own laws, that equality which thoſe calumniators denied they poſſeſſed: to ſee even Jacobins taking refuge under

der them, and protected : to fee that they were too
ftrong to be refifted by any power, and too impartial to make any diftinction in perfons. Reflect
upon this, my countrymen ! Compare it with what
has juft paffed in France, where, after feven years
wafted in confufion, mifery, war and bloodfhed,
to attain Liberty and Equality, a Government is
at laft confolidated, which authorifes five men to
fend off, in tranfportation, its beft citizens, the
fuppofed legal organs and reprefentatives of the
people, without trial, and of courfe without crime.
Keep this ftill in your eye : it is worth a million of
abftract fpeculations on the fubjects of government
and moral conduct.   No end, however good, fay
the moralifts, can juftify bad means : accomplifhing bad ends by bad means, then, is furely the
higheft excefs of moral turpitude.   I am difpofed
to believe, that in politics, as well as morals, the
better maxim would be, that the end attained by
bad means, cannot be good.   It would at leaft be
a good rule for the regulation of moral conduct ;
and I am fure it is founded in truth.   For as foon
will the deadly nightfhade exude manna from its
leaves, as moral evil produce moral good, or
murder and robbery end in freedom and good
government.

You

You muſt obſerve, that the firſt propoſition advanced by our Jacobins, in imitation of thoſe of France, was, that the will of the people only, that is to ſay, the will of a *majority of the* people, could rightfully conſtitute government or law.—After induſtriouſly preaching and diſſeminating this doctrine, and ſcattering it through the country, enforced with all the ingenuity and eloquence of Mr. Paine, (who, by the bye, inſiſted that we had no conſtitution at all) they found, to their unſpeakable mortification, that the people of England had too much ſenſe to be caught by traps, ſo very clumſily baited; and that they not only recognized, but formally expreſſed unfeigned, zealous attachment and gratitude to their Conſtitution, and indignation againſt its enemies. The Jacobins then changed their tone, but without lowering their key; and broached a new doctrine, viz. that a majority of the people was not the legitimate ſource of government;—that the people could not, by any act of their own, diveſt themſelves of their inherent rights; and that if there were only ſeven men in the country in favour of thoſe rights, and the reſt of ſeven millions againſt them, it was treaſon in the majority (however large) to controvert them. Here were two principles, ſo contradictory in terms, that no caſuiſtry could reconcile them, made

F   the

the pretext by one and the fame body of men, for one and the fame line of conduct. However, as if it were to quafh all contention on fuch futile fubjects, the Directory, (thofe profound doctors of the French code, thofe fellows of the political College of Paris, the Alma Mater of Infurrection and the Rights of Man,) have practically evinced, in their late tranfactions, that neither the will of the people, nor the rights of the people, fhall avail againft the fuperiour wifdom of five men, and the fuperiour integrity and patriotifm of a ftanding army.

Are you not able now to determine, whether the Rights of Man, &c. was a true principle, or a pretext; or can you be any longer at a lofs to decide upon the views of its profeffors?

To throw a clearer light upon the fubject, and give you a deeper infpection of their bofoms, it will be neceffary to call to your recollection a few leading tranfactions.

Every party that gained poffeffion of the ruling power in France, was, in its turn, the object of our Jacobins' homage and affection—each till it was cut off; then our Jacobins configned it to execration,

execration, and transferred their fealty to the fuc-
ceffors.

When the Regicides triumphed over the King,
and the laft remnant of order and authority in
France, nothing could equal the tranfport of our
Jacobins. On that day, when the final fate and
execution of Louis was announced in London, one
might, with little fkill in phyfiognomy, have diftinguifhed the Jacobins by their faces—at all times
down-caft, gloomy and fierce, from inceffant medi-
tation upon murder, the grim joy that then gliftened
in their eyes, rendered them fuperlatively hideous.—
They fcarcely refrained from ftopping paffengers in
the ftreet to communicate the happy tidings.—
All the honourable murderers of antiquity hid
their diminifhed heads when compared with thofe
who had murdered Louis. Briffot was a God—
Roland an angel—as to Condorcet, Ariftotle,
Bacon, Newton and Franklin, were fchoolboys to
him: and Marat was another Brutus. Here the
parallel was clofeft, if indeed Marat was not injured by the comparifon.

While they were yet exulting at the new-born happinefs of mankind, in having found fuch worthy and
puiffant affertors of their rights—while yet their *te*

diabolum

diabolum for the murder of the King, and the ecstatic eulogies of his murderers were flaming on their brimstone lips, comes Robespierre, and sweeps away at once those gods, angels and philosophers.

" ———in the blossom of their sins,
" Unhousel'd, unanointed, unanelled:
" —No reckoning made, but sent to their account,
" With all their imperfections on their head."

The wind being changed, our Jacobins, with their accustomed fidelity, veered about too. *Robespierre* was declared to be the Salvation of France, and *the Guardian of the human race.*—And, horrible to relate ! his enormities, which I need not repeat, were justified upon the necessity of the case; and said to be necessary to the rights of man, to liberty and equality, and to the republic one and indivisible.

Robespierre fell—the Jacobins again rejoiced— it was massacre—no matter whether of friend or foe—it was massacre, revolution, and change of property, and Jacobins must approve of it. In twelve hours after he had been warmly panegyrized by our Jacobins, for having murdered some hundred thousand of his fellow citizens, his successors were panegyrized by the same Jacobins for mur-
dering

dering him; and Tallien's bombaftical invocation of the buft of Brutus was fpouted by twenty mouths at once, in every ale-houfe, gin-fhop, or club-room, from St. Catherine's to Seven Dials.

To conclude—*rights of man*, liberty and equality, majority of the people, and will of the people, and all the different dialects of that filthy jargon, are now compleatly overwhelmed and merged in the tyranny of the Directory.—And lo! the Jacobins are fatisfied: and why? Becaufe, though the form of their principle is deftroyed, the fubftance, that is to fay, the right of infurrection, plunder, and affaffination, not only remain untouched, but are fortified by a new precedent. It is very remarkable, that the only inftance of affaffination, regretted by Jacobins, was that of Marat. It was not extenfive enough to atone, by its grandeur, for the lofs of a Jacobin; and, what was worfe, it was attended with no revolution, no confifcation, no robbery; in fhort, it was fo much labour loft.

And here I cannot but relate a fact of a very curious kind, not a little characteriftical of this abandoned fect. Some time in 1793, a report prevailed, and was credited, that the glorious Wafhington

Wafhington had been affaffinated : a Jacobin, who was prefent when the report was mentioned, exclaimed, " That's right ! that's right ! I have for " fome time fufpected that Wafhington"——— " Good God ! how can you fay fo," faid a gentleman, who was prefent; " it was but yefterday I " heard you praife Wafhington, in a ftrain ap- " proaching to idolatry." " It may be fo," replied the Jacobin, " but he is affaffinated, you " know, and *of courfe* deferved it."

To wind up the whole, recollect the wicked and audacious attempt made upon the facred perfon of your Sovereign, all the refult of the plan of Jacobins, affembled at Chalk Farm. Recollect the attempts that were made to corrupt your army, and the formidable mutiny introduced into your fleet, in order to give France the afcendant.— Combine all thofe facts together, and hefitate, if you can, to pronounce, that thofe men are at enmity with your King, your Conftitution, your property, and your rights—that they feek your deftruction—that they are fworn to be enemies of mankind, and that that is the only oath they will fail to break. If not in their hoftility to England, how will you account for their uniform approbation, and zealous defence of all the contradictory

clafhing

clashing events and interests which have succeeded each other in France?

Those are the people who most vehemently urge you to sue for peace in any tone, however abject, of humiliation :—those are they who most loudly and pertinaciously call for parliamentary reform.—Although the resolutions of their committees are yet extant, in which they insist, that parliament, in agitating and agreeing to a reform, would be guilty of an act of usurpation.

Having dispatched one side, let us proceed to the other, and examine the claims of those who urge you to prosecute the war in maintainance of your honour and existence : you will then estimate their comparative weight in the scale of impartial reason.

At the head of these is your gracious Sovereign —————— ————— to call in question or discuss his right to direct you—his claims upon your affection —his zeal for the welfare of his dominions and subjects, would be abominable. You know them; you feel them; you confess them. It is as impossible the king of England can be indifferent to your interests, as that he should be regardless of
his

his own honour, his fame, his exiftence, or his happinefs. They are infeparably connected. They
are wedded never to be divorced.

But the King, you will fay, may be mifadvifed:—
he may;—but you will be able to judge whether
he is mifadvifed in this inftance, when you confider
who they are that advife, and go along with him,
in the profecution of the war: they are the lords
and commons of parliament, with very few excep-
tions: they are thofe who have a permanent landed
property in the country: the fober, the affluent, the difcreet, the wife, and the honeft: thofe
whofe interefts are rooted in the foil of England,
and interwoven with your own, and whofe profperity, and that of their children, muft neceffarily
be co-equal, and co-exiftent, with the profperity
of England. Men, who cannot boaft of being
citizens of the world, becaufe no part of the world
but England would afford them maintenance.
Balance thofe againft men who, exclufive of their
actual hoftility, are here only tenants at will: who,
having no goods or chattles to encumber them in
their migration, can flit like a fhadow, from region to region: who have no affection but to
themfelves; no attachments but to their own interefts: who can lap up their wardrobe in a hand-
kerchief,

kerchief, and as they walk to Paris, can truly chirp along the road, " *Omnia mea, mecum porto.*" Balance them, I say, and decide—decide between unprincipled indigence, that would fuck your blood on the one hand, and the whole wifdom, virtue, and property of the country on the other.

I reafon with you, you obferve, as if the alternative of peace or war lay in your option; and I do fo, that your will may go hand in hand with your ne-cefiity; but it muft, neverthelefs, not be concealed from you, that if you were defirous of peace, you could not obtain it on lower terms than unconditional fubjection to France, and the difruption of Ireland from the British empire. Are you ready to agree to thefe conditions?—Remember, the whole power of France is turned to effect the ruin of this country, and *Delenda eft Carthago*, is infcribed on her ftandards. Roufe from your lethargy, exert yourfelves, and you may yet make her the Carthage, and be yourfelves the Romans.

You cannot now be at a lofs what determination to come to. If your own obfervation of the plans of France did not point out the necefiity of vigo-rous refiflance, you might infer it from the eager-nefs with which the Jacobins would perfuade you,

to

to fly into her confuming embraces. It is not more certain, that you ought to deprecate peace, fince it is defired by the Jacobins, than that you ought to fufpect the Jacobins for defiring peace: and if your own reafon and perfonal fafety did not urge you to refiftance, the advice, the opinion, and co-operation of the king, the parliament, and the bulk of the property, and virtue of the country, united in one caufe, muft be enough to ftimulate to action, and fill you with courage and confidence.

The whigs who from error, fome perhaps from party rancour, have all along difputed the expediency of the war; but who are, neverthelefs, little difpofed to fubmit to French enchroachment, will agree that force muft be oppofed to force; but they will fay, " change your minifters; what " can you hope from men, whofe conduct in the " war has been fo weak, fo erroneous, and fo un- " fuccefsful ?"

To deny that there have been errors, in the conduct of the war, would be to forfeit all pretenfions to truth and common fenfe. But before you go fo far as to defire a change, confider well what probability there is of your getting a better adminiftration. Of the complicated injuftice with

2   which

which minifters are always treated, there is no part more glaring or abfurd than that of condemning them for mifcarriages in war : in every conteft one fide or other muft neceffarily mifcarry, and no events in life are fo much under the direction of chance, as thofe of war. The accident of a moment, events which cannot be forefeen, or if forefeen, could not be obviated, may determine the fate of a campaign. In a doubtful field, a fingle fhot may turn the fortune of the day. For wilful neglect, or for corruption, if proved, a minifter is refponfible; but furely not for bare mifcarriage. I prefume you will hardly fufpect his Majefty's minifters of betraying their own caufe, or felling victories to the enemy. Have you any reafon to believe there are men ready to fucceed them, more zealous in the country's caufe, more capable of conducting the war, or more fitted in all refpects for their office ? It would be unjuft to compare any fet of men who have ever exifted, with the prefent minifters, fince no men at any period, or in any country, ever had fuch difficulties to encounter. In no war or country but this were minifters obliged to face the enemy in the gate, and bear the poifoned fhafts of traitors in the rear; they are the only minifters who held the reins of government at a period and in a country, where

G 2   parties

parties were permitted openly to efpoufe the enemy. At no time, and in no country, was the progrefs of public affairs impeded, the weaknefs of the country expofed, the pregnable parts pointed out to the enemy, or the operations of government traverfed for the purpofes of expofure, to the fame extent as they are now by the unbridled licentioufnefs of certain daily prints. The anticipating malignity of jacobins, will not fuffer them to confine their accufations and charges againft the minifters, to what they *have* done, but they actually accufe them of what they *will* do, before it is done. Thus, well knowing (for their information of certain things is good—*ob caufas*) well knowing that the French government had no intention of making peace on fuch terms as England could accept, they inceffantly tortured the public fight with pitiful paragraphical fuggeftions that our minifters were not fincere in negociation, but only playing off a farce to amufe the people. But why, in God's name, or to what end?—are minifters fuch abject fools? Do they know fo little of the human heart as to be ignorant that a temporary deception of that kind would aggravate the temper of the people by difappointment? Is not your enemy informed every day, through the medium of fome of our prints, of things
which,

which, whether true or falſe, muſt tend to inhance her demands in negociation? And is no allowance to be made to miniſters for all thoſe diſadvantages?

At all times change is doubtful in its effects: At this time it would be peculiarly hazardous:—it is no time for innovation of any kind. What good ſeaman would wiſh to ſhift the helms-man in a heavy ſquall? Beſides, it would on other accounts be a great misfortune to loſe our miniſters now. Even their miſcarriages have contributed to enrich their minds with knowledge and experience, and fit them for a further conteſt; after having paid for their experience, it would be fooliſh to diſmiſs them without reaping the fruits of it, and more ſo to take in their ſtead, raw inexperience to go through its noviciate, and ruin the country; have you any grave and cogent reaſon to believe that if the helm had been in other hands, the veſſel would not have foundered long ago? I believe not.

But while you regret a few partial miſcarriages, do not forget the number and ſplendor of your victories.—While you lament the error of ſending to the Weſt Indies the troops that ought to have reinforced and ſupplied the brave men of *Le Vendee*, be not unmindful that the predominance of your power

power in thofe iflands was eftablifhed by that error.
Recollect that your armies have loft no honour,
and that your navy has been irrefiftable; that the
Eaft Indies, and its wealth and commerce, have
been made almoft exclufively your own; fecure,
(unlefs in ignominious panic you negociate them
away) beyond the reach of accident. Remember
that this war has put your navy (the natural defence of England) upon a footing beyond the
dreams of the moft fanguine, and abfolutely an-
nihilated thofe of France, Spain, and Holland.
Meafure thefe with the advantages gained in any
other war, and you will find that they deride all
comparifon. And will you then be fo loft to all
fenfe of juftice as to concur in the condemnation of
thofe minifters who gained them; or to all fenfe of
national pride, as to agree to their being yielded
up, to purchafe the ruin and ignominy of a peace
with the doctrine of infurrection and regicide?

The fate of great geniufes, (fays Pope) is like
that of great minifters, though they are confeffedly
the firft in the commonwealth, they muft be en-
vied, and calumniated only for being at the head
of it. Perfons whofe affairs are in great diforder,
feldom look out for the true authors of their mif-
fortunes, but difcharge their fpleen upon thofe
moft

moft obvious to view; and the fot, whofe profli-
gacy brings him to beggary, and the merchant
who ruins himfelf by foolifh fpeculations, will
each alike charge the poverty of his family to the
mifconduct of minifters. Befides, it is natural that
public mifcarriages fhould occafion popular calumny, for to vulgar minds, (fays the greateft
modern philofopher—Burke) the only criterion of
wifdom is fuccefs. The people of England gall-
ing with the preffure of calamity, think only of
their prefent mifcarriages, forgetting that at the
commencement of the war, the prefent minifter
was their idol. Thus the laft accident gives co-
lour to all the reft, and ftamps the whole of a
man's conduct with misfortune or happinefs. And
hence we may infer what an uncertain criterion of
merit is popularity; fince it is often lavifhly beftowed where there is no merit, and often refufed
where it ought to be beftowed. But this, with
fome other fubjects on which I lightly touch now,
will be the fubject of another addrefs.

Having difcuffed the merits of jacobins, it is
now time to advert to thofe of their patrons and
patterns, the French—at all times, even in their
flavery, turbulent, intriguing, reftlefs, and fubject
to be puffed by every blaft of profperity, to an

ideal

ideal fize far beyond their real dimenfions, it might be forefeen that when flufhed with frequent victories, they could not poffibly make a mild or moderate ufe of their good fortune; but would on the contrary, as it has fince happened, abandon themfelves to jealoufies, intrigue, cabals, and ambition. As foon as they got loofe from the wholefome reftraint of their monarchy, the ftrongeft were immediately for governing, or crufhing, the weakeft; and as many flattered themfelves they were ftrongeft, their contentions were innumerable; whatever faction might have happened to poffefs the power to-day, the others looked to poffefs it to-morrow, or the next day, but all united in this one opinion, that war was neceffary to their particular views. So that fetting out with a view to afcertain their own liberties, they imperceptibly changed their fyftem to that of annoying their neighbours, and endeavouring to accomplifh the deftruction of all other governments, and particularly of this. Upon this plan they have uniformly acted, feizing and breaking fceptres at will, and out of the ruins of governments overturned, and kingdoms divided, erecting new republics at pleafure, enlifting the difcontented and factious of all countries as fpies, traitors, and infurgents, and affaulting their ene-

mies

mies with the joint forces of steel and jacobinism.
At length finding the most firm resistance to their
abominable plans, to be made by England, they are
resolved to wipe out the very name, or be undone.
Whether they shall succeed or not, depends upon
you, not them.

While France had the benefit of our jacobins here,
urging you to peace, in order to excite discontent,
she herself shuffled off the point with a degree of craft,
and effrontery that appears astonishing; always af-
ecting to be ready to negociate, but always resolved
not to conclude a peace. After the regicides had,
as was well predicted by Mr. Windham, in 1792,
conquered a great part of Europe, by *detail*, and
by an irrevocable law of their own, annexed so
much of those conquests to their republic, as the
powers of Europe would not, nor could with safety,
have permitted their monarchs to retain, our ministers, compelled by the clamours for peace,
wickedly raised by the jacobins, and foolishly
echoed by the whigs, offered to negociate at Basle—
their overtures were insolently rejected. It is not
a long time since such an insult would of itself
have been thought by Englishmen a sufficient cause
for war, or reparation. Still urged by repeated
clamours, the ministers dispatched Lord Malmesbury to Paris; and an English ambassador was for

H   th

the firſt time ſeen *begging* for peace in France;
having completely entrapped you into this degrada-
tion, they amuſed themſelves for a while with his
Lordſhip, and on a ſudden, to finiſh your diſgrace,
ordered him away, rather with the indignity due to a
ſpy, than with the decency which ought to be ob-
ſerved to the ambaſſador of a great empire. Had
all parties conſpired to elevate the jacobins, to flatter
the pride of France, and humble England, they
could not more effectually have done it. But was that
the fault of miniſters? No, it was their misfortune, and they felt it. After all this, a third attempt was made at Liſle, where Lord Malmeſbury
again underwent probation, and was again inſolently
diſmiſſed, without cauſe aſſigned, or any obvious mo-
tive, but that of purſuing the war to your extermi-
nation. They agreed to negotiate, only to add another indignity to thoſe they had already offered you,
and to break the pride and ſpirit of Britain.

See then the diſgrace and humiliation into which
an impatient, inglorious deſire for peace has brought
you!! It has accumulated inſult upon inſult, and
created many cauſes for war, when there ought to be
but one; for every one of thoſe indignities ſhould
be wiped away by a ſeparate act of reparation.

Were

Were you to look back in the history of England, no farther than the prefent century, you would find examples to make you exult at the noble bearing of your fathers, and blufh at your own degeneracy.—Was the incroachment of Spain on the Falkland Iflands, a place in a very diftant part of South America, the poffeffion of which, may be of the value of about one fhilling, not more, to England; was that an object to be compared, for importance, with the flighteft of the manifold aggreffions and infults, heaped upon you by the regicide ufurpations of France? Was the annexation of Corfica to the crown of France, fo important to Great Britain, as the conqueft of the Netherlands, the opening of the Scheldt, the attack upon Holland, or the decree of fraternization?—furely not; and yet England, in both cafes, was in a flame, at the tardinefs of our court to refent them; and the wifdom and temper of the executive government, were never more feverely tafked than in keeping down the bold intrepid fpirit of the country, and allaying the ferment of public indignation. And here let me remind you of the noble, generous ardour with which you yourfelves entered on the prefent war. The atrocities of France were then new to you—you fympathifed with the oppreffed—you

turned

turned with appropriate horror from the oppreſſors—
and you gallantly raiſed your arm to keep the fiend
regicide from your ſhores.—And has habit yet ſo
hardened you to thoſe atrocities, that you ceaſe to lament them? Has oppreſſion changed its nature ſince,
or have its features grown ſo familiar to your ſight,
as to loſe their deformity? Has time reconciled
you to regicide? Or has the *penitence*, the *ſincere
humiliation* of the offenders, done away their of-
fence? What is that particular event in the war,
which ſeems to have expiated, to your feelings, all
thoſe abominations that firſt rouſed your ſpirit into
the honeſt promptitude with which you undertook
it? Is it becauſe the enemy has pledged himſelf to
follow up the war, to your extinction, that your
ardour abates, and your alacrity ſlackens? Or,
ſince the motives to war, and the neceſſity for op-
poſing France, have increaſed every day from
the commencement, till now, they are become
inevitable, why do you not call forth all your
energy?

The inſults you have received within this year,
are of themſelves ample grounds for war. Even
Mr. Fox allows that the honour of a nation is one of
the moſt juſtifiable grounds of war. If the meaneſt
individual

individual among you is infulted, will he not refent
it? will he not fight even to the death?—why fhould
he, for an infult, a breath of air, endanger his own
life, and endeavour to take away that of a fellow
creature? He will fay, his honour, his reputation,
his character demand it. And fhall an individual
be prefumptuous enough to think fame, character
and honour, more neceffary to himfelf than to the
ftate, of which he forms but a very inconfiderable
fraction?—or do you fuppofe that you can preferve
your perfonal honour while your country is difgraced?—if you do, you are a difgrace not only to
your country, but to human nature. But the cafe
is much ftronger on behalf of the country; for it is
criminal in an individual to fight his fellow citizen,
though a vicious cuftom prick him on; and it is incumbent on every country to vindicate her honour
by war. And I will tell you why:—fuch is the pro-
fligacy of human nature, that infult, tamely fubmitted
to, breeds contempt, and contempt encourages injury; now in the cafe of an individual, if his patience
under infult, fuperinduces an injury, the law will redrefs him; but in the cafe of nations, there is no law,
no redrefs, but force: a nation, therefore, muft ftop
the injury in its incipient ftage—the infult. Hence
you will conclude then how much more incumbent

it

it is on you, to revenge the infult offered to your country, than to refent that offered to yourfelves.

Perhaps you flatter yourfelves that the French would be lenient and generous in victory, liberal in their terms of peace, and fincere in adherence to them.—For their lenity, their generofity, and their fincerity, look to thofe places they have conquered, where you will fee them written in blood and tears:—as to their terms, the bare mention of them, would either fet you mad with rage, or melancholy with defpair. As one fmall fpecimen of them; what do you think of the feparation of Ireland from this country? Guefs the reft!! Look to the Netherlands, Savoy, Italy, Germany, Geneva, and America, and then judge which is worfe, the fraternity of France or hoftility. Where treaties or neutrality forbid guns or bayonets, intrigue and infurrection fupply their place; and where French armies cannot go, French principles do their office. Have you witneffed their progrefs—their conduct to all ftates—their modes of enriching themfelves from all—and do you not tremble? If there exifted a heart fo impenetrable, to whom fuch a fcene could be a matter of indifference, the pencil of Hogarth never fketched off a more lu-

dicrous

dicrous exhibition, than the progrefs of a French
army, through an unrefifting fraternized country. Oh
if that prince of fatirifts were alive now, to paint
General Buonaparte traverfing Italy, at the head
of his gaunt crew, like a jew-broker crying for
caft cloaths, picking up, for want of better, every
rag that offers--ftanding like a relentlefs com-
pounding landlord, at the doors of the Italian
huts, extolling his own generofity for not ex-
acting *all*, and loading carts with old pictures,
mufty feather beds, worm-eaten bed-pofts, rufh
chairs, deal tables, and leaky pots and kettles, to
fend to Paris in triumph:—Good God ! if pity did
not exact our tears, and tell us it was criminal to
fmile, what a rich field for ridicule it would be, to fee
the generals of the republic plundering where they
were bound to protect, and in every action, from fighting a battle down to dancing a rigadoon, illuftrating
that whimfical compound of ludicrous and cruel, that
nauceous mixture of ape and tiger, in which the
French were fo happily characterifed by Voltaire :
—extending their war plunder down to theft—
their theft to childifh folly :—carrying off church
bells, and filching pictures, bronzes, butterflies,
and pieces of virtu :—in a negociation for a fubfidy
of millions, bargaining for a *Cameo*, or a Buft ;

and converting a treaty for a province into a broker's or chandler's bargain, in which a picture more or lefs is thrown in to make the weight :— marching an army two or three hundred miles, to enforce the requifition of a RAPHAEL ;— and bribed to divert a march, from its direct rout, with a timely offer of a Baptift's Head by Guido, or a Venus by Carlo Morat. From the ferocity and meannefs, from the fternnefs and caprice of fuch men, what could you hope, if you trufted to their lenity, or moderation. In one man, in one hour, (fuch is the compafs of their caprice) you may ftrike every note in the two gamuts of folly and ferocity ; from the cutting of a throat in one, to the cutting of a caper in the other. Murder, rape, inceft, robbery; tumbling, capering, fiddling, and buffoonery :—fighting and pimping :—riding the war-horfe, and combing a lap-dog :—all between fun-rife and fun-fet. Is it in the morals, in the moderation, in the fteadinefs, the confiflency, the fortitude, or the equanimity of fuch men you would expect to find generous conquerors ?—No, no, my Countrymen ! they muft be kept off—they muft be convinced that England is not fo very eafy a conqueft as they expect to find her ; and if they will not hearken to reafon, they muft be taught it from the mouths of your

cannon.

cannon. In contact with them there is no fecurity;—they muft be kept off;—truft them not;—
give the war effective force,—give to it yourfelves,
and your means:—there is no paltering—no medium—feeding the lamp with fcanty drops will but
confume the wick;—fill it full, or your light is extinguifhed for ever.

Do you not fee that the Directory of France are
fo circumftanced, that they cannot make peace
with regard to their own fafety? If they difband
the army, the people will then eftablifh a government of their own liking, which they have
now plainly fhewn to be monarchy with fome li-
mitations; and the Directory will perifh, perhaps
on the fcaffold:—If they do not difband it, they
will live like the Turkifh Viziers, or the old Ro-
man Emperors, in conftant fear of, and dependance on their foldiery,—their Prætorian guards—or
their Janiffaries—call them which you will. They
will, therefore, by all poffible means, endeavour
to protract the war, in order to find the army in
work and in food:—in that cafe they would certainly think London excellent head quarters; and
after all, it is not clear that Monf. Buonaparte
would not as lief load a cart with gold, filver,

jewellery,

jewellery, cloathing, &c. &c. in Cheapſide, Fleet Street, or the Strand, as with the fineſt *Titiaa's*, or *Michael Angelo's* in Italy.

No, my countrymen, neither peace, nor juſtice, nor equity, are the objects of the French—war only is their object, and they can ſupport war only by foreign plunder. Do you think that your cla-mours for peace will accelerate its attainment, or your humiliation ſecure you from plunder?—Encou-raged by your ſolicitations France grows bolder— and aſks you with a ſneer, " Can you expect me " to make peace while Ireland is diſaffected, and " you are ſo averſe to ſupport the war?" You will find her every day more inacceſſible to reaſon, more ſteeled againſt remorſe,—more regardleſs of law, mercy, good faith, and integrity; you will find her irreſiſtable, and inevitable, if you do not meet her with your cannon charged to the mouth. Avoid, then, ſoliciting for peace as you would ſhun perdi-tion;—conſider the effect it will have—not only will it render peace more difficult of attainment, but accelerate another war, before you have re-covered from the waſte of this; while your arma-ments will all be diſbanded. The reſtleſs heart of France, turgid with the pride of victory, and ele-

vated

vated upon the humiliation of England—inflated, overbearing, and infolent, will be fatisfied with nothing fhort of the fubjection of yourfelves, the demolition of your commerce, the fall of your navy—and, to accomplifh thofe objects, will foon enter upon another war, with the promptitude and firm ftep of confcious fuperiority.

In fuch circumftances, will you not endeavour to roufe yourfelves? the danger of refiftance is nothing compared with that of fubmiffion. Will you then fink into the fatal panic of thofe poltroon foldiers, who rather face the death of a court-martial, becaufe remote, than rifk the fhot of the enemy in the field?—Far, far from Englifhmen be fuch infamy.

There are fome who will fay, " Yes, we ought " to defend ourfelves, and we would, but the ex- " pence is more than we can bear." Good God! So if any one would offer to find fufficient funds for the war, without touching your purfes, and thus endeavour to reconcile your duty with your avarice, you would acknowledge the neceffity, and defend your Country. Your Country! Why?— Becaufe your Country is, in fact, your property. See the abfurdity; you will venture your life for

the

the defence of your property, but yet would rather give up the whole of that property to the violence and force of an enemy, than a part of it for the security of the whole. And are you really so forlorn as to hope you will be able to reconcile pleasure with necessity, security with sloth, energy or courage with voluptuousness, or honour with submission? Do you hope to preserve your money, by hoarding it in dormant store for the allurement of robbers; or would you be silly enough to think of intimidating a highwayman who demanded your purse, by telling him you had the money in your pocket with which you *might* have bought a pistol?

How many bitter remembrances of what England once was, and what, alas! she now is;—of her deplorable fall from manhood, to disgraceful effeminacy, do we meet in our streets!—What do we see? Even while the cannon of the enemy thunder on our shores—beings—men—not women, but something at least bearing the shape of men, muscular and brawny as Irish chairmen, not ashamed to linger and lounge at home, leading a lazy and sauntering life, strutting in silk stockings, pantaloons, and powdered heads, from the door of a

shop

ſhop to the counter, and from the counter to the
door, grinning ſoft bewitchment at the paſſing
ladies ; meaſuring tape, ribbands, and bobbin, and
eating the bread of the diligent, the laborious, and
the productive. Gabbling politics, God wot ; aſk-
ing for news ; vapouring, cenſuring, and calumniating their protectors, while the very ſuggeſtion
of ſelf-defence, makes them tremble like a hurt
wild duck at the report of a gun.

We ſee worſe ;—The affluent, who having more
at ſtake, ſhould be more alarmed, whiſtling thought-
leſsly along, making their wealth, which ought to
be the ſtrength of their country, its weakneſs ;
detracting from its armed defence, and from its
productive labour, by filling their houſes with a
gang of that moſt contemptible, uſeleſs, and as
inſolent as uſeleſs, band of bipeds, called footmen :—
Revelling away at their eaſe, like Falſtaff in his inn,
regardleſs of the heavy reckoning that is to follow :—
protecting and countenancing abuſes, becauſe they
afford pleaſure and gratify vanity :—evincing their
liberty and rights, by forging their own gold into
fetters for their own legs ; and refuſing to do what
they ought, merely to ſhew they can do what they
pleaſe :—drowning all recollection of the honourable

inheritance

inheritance of their anceftors, and of their own fame, in oblivious draughts of pleafure; and, like failors enfrenzied with liquor and defpair in a finking fhip, abandoning all meafures of fafety, drinking deep of intoxication, and dreffing themfelves in gold lace and finery, to go down in ftate. Indeed, when the felfifh referve, the avarice, the voluptuoufnefs and obftinate fupinenefs in this hour of danger of the rich is confidered, we cannot fo much wonder that thofe whom poverty renders difcontented, fhould liften to the foft tale of the ferpent, and fwallow the apple of deftruction.

If I were fpeaking to your fathers, I would fpeak thus: " Britons! if you had the fecurity of " Heaven for the fincerity of the French, and a " promife that they would ftop where they are, " and no more moleft you, yet I call God to " witnefs, you will be unworthy the name of " Britons, if, for the fake of debafing repofe, you " fuffer your fame to be tarnifhed, and the he- " reditary honours, derived from your anceftors, " to be trampled under foot." Such a fpeech would thrill to their hearts; but to you, who rarely value honour but as it happens to be an appendage to wealth, it will be a fubject of derifion.

Whence

Whence arises this paffive difpofition, fo unlike your fathers?—whence this fhameful falling off?—from France. From the attempts of her agents and imitators here, to get at the pure fountains of honour and liberty, and pollute them with blood and licentioufnefs. You imagine you fee their currents ftained, and fear to tafte. Wall them in—make a rampart round them with your bodies—let not the peftilent breath of Frenchman or jacobin taint them: and you will find that their influence upon your conduct will be like magic.

Good God! caft your eyes inward, view yourfelves as in a mirror, fee what a fpectacle you Englifhmen now prefent to view—openly and repeatedly infulted, you are tame—injured, indolent—menaced, cowardly—on the verge of ruin, flothful, funk in apathy, and nervelefs. Skulking into your huts, fhrinking in trepidation from the thunder ftorm, and each comforting himfelf with the hope that the bolt will mifs him:—refigning yourfelves to phlegmatic defpair or indifference, and finking, like Dutch failors in a tempeft, with your hands in your pockets;—while your internal enemies, no lefs than your foreign, (in order to encourage and give you a pretext for this fupinenefs, and to divert you from

from the difcovery of the important truth, that you
are the perfons injured) tell you that the war is a
war for the king, and not for you.—Wicked fub-
tlety, and fatal credulity!—pernicious diftinction!
and more pernicious blindnefs!! Your caufe is
the caufe of the King—he has no other caufe but
yours; for your happinefs and protection he un-
dertakes the labours, and endures the care and fo-
licitude of war. What benefit, in God's name, can
war be to him?—Certainly none.—Spurn from
you thofe dangerous vipers who tell you the re-
verfe; be affured that merit, and only merit, is
the object of their calumny—it was fo at all times;
the moft virtuous men were always the victims of
Republican calumny. The glorious Pericles was
the perpetual object of Republican libellers—wretches
fo mean as to have no title to remembrance, but the
infamous diftinction of abufing the beft man in
the world. The god-like Socrates himfelf was
condemned to death in a Republic by the li-
bellous arts of Ariftophanes, a defpicable Come-
dian. In both cafes, the people who liftened to
the libels were as criminal as the libellers themfelves. Seeing then the evils that muft follow your
liftening to fuch deluders, it will be folly and ftupi-
dity or vice not to pufh them from you with abhor-
rence.

But

But you will afk, " What is to be done?" I will tell you.

Firft, fet it down as an axiom, that France (by which I mean its ufurpers) is your irreconcileable enemy. Nothing but a firm perfuafion of this can fave you.

Next put your whole truft in Government; ftrengthen it with your voice, your arm, and your purfe. Proclaim to the world, and to your enemies in particular, that your Government is the Government of your choice, and of your opinion; and that you will ftand or fall with it. This will be worth a million of foldiers.

Reverence and confide in thofe who recommend vigorous meafures; and diftruft thofe who flatter your floth with indulgence. Look on all thofe as enemies who infidioufly remind you of your rights, and all thofe as friends who remind you of your duties. Be affured, that he who boldly tells you of your duty, would be among the firft to vindicate your rights. Remember that rights and duties are infeperable, and operate as mutual caufe and effect. Every right creates a correfpondent duty, and out

K   of

of the difcharge of your duties grow your rights:
every individual has a right to the protection of his
country, but it is his duty, in return, to con-
tribute his fhare to its defence. They who bid you
neglect your duties, only want to ftrip you of your
rights.

Shake off indolence, avarice, and luxury; fight,
or pay thofe who will; do both yourfelves, the
greater your praife; do neither, the greater your infamy.—Remember that a foft voluptuous life, un-
nerves the heart, extinguifhes the courage, enfeebles
the underftanding, and fafhions you for flaves.

Raife fupplies cheerfully; embody and fit yourfelves for action. I mean that of the field—not that
which you are faid to difplay in the tavern and the
fpouting club.

Look to your wealth as a curfe if you hoard it,
but a peculiar blefling, at this time, if rightly applied; fince it will enable you to fhun all the
horrors of France.—Confign a portion of it to the
maintenance of the war; if that will not fuffice,
give more, and more, and more; even all, rather
than yield it, your own lives, your wives, your

6   daughters,

daughters, and your country, to that devouring beaft, Jacobinifm.

Refolve on an *honourable and fecure* peace, or a continuation of the war; if the latter, let it be waged as England ought to wage it—with vigour and effect.

Keep a vigilant eye upon the Jacobins. France, without their aid, could never have brought you to the ftate you are in; but be juft and diftinguifh them from the whigs: you will know the former by their malignity to the king, by their combining his name, in converfation, with images of derifion or of murder; by their praife of the French, and by their enthufiaftic admiration of Brutus and thofe homicide *patriots* of antiquity, who facrificed friends, brothers and fathers at the fhrine of ideal liberty.— Thofe monfters whofe exiftence good men might yet doubt, if France did not exhibit them daily fpringing up in horrid fucceffion. Thofe terrific characters, whom Providence feems to have ordained to eafe the throes of our corrupt nature; and to ferve, in the moral, like volcanoes in the phyfical world, to difgorge its inbred wickednefs to the terror and aftonifhment of mankind.

Above

Above all things refift every attempt, whatever form it may affume, to promote difunion or create commotion in the country; poftpone to the day of peace and good temper, all queftions of change in the public polity. Let that of parliamentary reform reft for a while; a year or two will make no great difference; myfelf, an advocate for reform, I do not fee how it could at this time conduce to any good purpofe. A fhort delay is better than a dangerous experiment. Run your fhip into harbour before you attempt to repair; it would be madnefs to put her on the heel in a tempeft.

And tell Mr. F— that in withdrawing from the Houfe of Commons, he is guilty of an impofition on his conftituents; he has no right to defert the poft which they have intrufted to his vigilance— he has no difcretionary power in the matter;— attend he ought, or vacate his feat. It is a fhame and a folly fo openly to avow, that not the intereft of his conftituents, but his own, is the object of his going into parliament;—minifters fhould be vigilantly watched, not perpetually and indifcriminately oppofed.

Having

Having thus pointed out to you what you ought
to do, and why you ought to do it; little more
remains for me *at this time*, than to befeech you to
bring what I have faid home to your hearts. After
what you have heard of the French and the Jacobins,
of democracy and the Rights of Man, after what you
fee now tranfacting in France, are you ftill fo much
infatuated with them, as to give up your wealth,
your arts, your manufactures, your commerce, your
fleets, your every thing, perhaps your lives, to
compliment and enrich them, and their advocates.
The wife Lycurgus once faid to a man who excef-
fively praifed democracy, " go friend ! and fet it up
in your own houfe firft." As much as to fay, there
would then be as many mafters as fervants. Pre-
cious tyranny!!—No, my countrymen, true liberty,
in its purity and perfection, confifts in a well
grounded dependance upon juftice, which can only
be difpenfed and fecured by government legally
eftablifhed, and laws arifing gradually and flowly from
it, and from occafion ;—laws applied to the tempers
and harmonizing by habit and early inculcation,
with the feelings and mind of the people. Are
you prepared to yield up to a ftern and infolent foe,
the Conftitution of your wife forefathers, the
government of their choice, which by a kind of
mutual

mutual affimilation makes part of yourfelves;
which has grown with your growth, and ftrength-
ened with your ftrength; for which your gallant
anceftors fhed their blood in torrents; under which
you have grown great and opulent; and made this
little bleak ifland the miftrefs of the world—that
Conftitution which, to ufe the words of Addifon,
" makes your barren rocks and your bleak moun-
tains fmile;" and has enabled you to cover the whole
face of the globe with wealth, wrung from the
reluctant hand of nature; and with power that once
derided refiftance. Are you prepared to caft your-
felf in the duft and lick the feet of your ferocious
adverfary? or are you fo blinded by the artifices
of his agents, as not to perceive that the horrible
tragedy which has deluged Europe with blood, is
advancing to its cataftrophe; and that the laft fcene
will be laid in England, if you do not drive the
actors off the ftage? Will you, while peril and defo-
lation ftalk around your coafts, liften to the traitors
who flatter your inclinations, and humour your
weaknefs, only to put you off your guard, and
make you the inftruments of your own ruin: while
thofe who fpend fleeplefs nights and days of anguifh
in your fervice, endure the weight of your obloquy,
and

and senseless reproach. Turning from your physi-
cian, you prescribe for yourselves and swallow
poison. Disgrace will accumulate upon disgrace; the
country will be reduced to a province, yourselves
to beggary; your reputation will wither, your name
be for ever polluted; while those wretches will sing
io triumphe, in the camps of the French, deride
your credulity, hug themselves in self-applause,
on the traffic they have made, and with a sneer
remind you, that you were the contrivers of your
own ruin.

But why this incessant clamour for peace? Do
you think the king and his ministers are not as
much disposed to enjoy the blessings of peace as
you can be? Are they not a little more interested
in it, than the Jacobins who raise the shout against
war, only to kill the manly spirit of the nation? Do
you reflect—can you combine—can you distin-
guish? Why does your excellent government decline
a peace? Because the enemy will not afford it on
any terms short of disgrace, ruin and subjection.
Why do the Jacobins urge it? for the same reason.

Cannot

Cannot you fee all this? Cannot you perceive that the French ufurpers, knowing you are able to give them more trouble than the whole world befides, are fighting, caballing, treating, and intriguing with all Europe, and tampering with your own people, to procure your extinction; that it is the ultimate object of their views, and that they are bent upon accomplifhing it; what can you do then but act the part of Britons, and fight it out with them? Your ruin is inevitable, if on the one hand you do not oppofe force to force, and on the other they will allow you no refpite. Your navy will be deftroyed, your manufactures vanifh; (they will not be allowed time to decay) and the commerce that now fwells the tide of the Thames, the Severn, and your other rivers, will pafs over, and fill the ports of your enemy; and to compleat the meafure of your woes, the fcenes which have difgraced and deluged with blood the kingdom of France, will be performed here, for you have among you Robefpierres, Carrieres and Collot d'Herbois in numbers, ready to ftep upon the ftage and act the fame bloody tragedy. Oh what a change! Oh what a revolution! The French, lately poor, fquallid, unimportant, without commerce or confequence, will become the arbiters of the world;

while

while you will yield up all your glories for obfcurity—your luxury for want—and your affluence, pride and fplendor, for bankruptcy, beggary and fhame.—Defpifed, abandoned, forgotten, the very remnants of your former comfort will be torn from your backs, by gallic foldiers ; and the miferable, tawdry, pantaloon rags, of your tawny conquerors will be fhifted, *with all that them inherit*, from their lean fhirtlefs carcafes, to decorate you for their triumph, and give the finifhing ftroke to your humiliation.

Accurfed be that day when avarice drove ambition from England, and luxury fupplanted old britifh honour and hardihood. Why were your fathers great and illuftrious ? becaufe they were lefs voluptuous than proud—becaufe they loved glory more than wealth, and were jealous of their honour ; honour, the ftrongeft out-work of fafety : while wealth faps it, or rather acts the traitor, who opens the gates, and betrays the citadel to to the enemy. Be not deceived ! the tempeft increafes ; prepare to encounter it ; do not play the idiot, but fhake from your heart, and throw overboard thofe cumbrous trappings of voluptuoufnefs, which already fink you fo deep, elfe you inevitably perifh. Your

L   fumptuous

sumptuous houses, your plate, your horses, your
carriages, your useless or rather pernicious herds of
footmen, lining your halls dozens deep, will be contemptible baubles to take in barter for your fame,
your honour, and your country's good. But what
must be your feelings if, loving them so much
as to purchase them at that ignominious price,
you should in the end lose them also? And lose
them you must, if you do not exert yourselves;
hasten then to do your duty; devote yourself
for a time to the defence of your country; bestow a part of that which you melt in luxury,
parade, and vice, in circulating ruinous and extrava-
gant fashions, in giving sanction to prodigality, in
corrupting female innocence, and in fantastic follies,
that leave only stings behind them, bestow it, I say,
on the general safety. If you do not, you are
undone; panic never dreamt of such horrors as are
in store for you, if neglecting this admonition you
resign yourself to voluptuous apathy and inaction.
It is no time to sleep, you are tottering on the brink
of a precipice, and nothing but immediate retro-
grade motion can save you; to stand or to move
onward in your present direction are alike dangerous
—for whether you leap forward, or the ground
crumbles away from under you, your fate is the
same—*You fall never to rise again.*

FINIS.